How to Use This Book

Writing an argument is different than persuasive writing. Persuasive writing requires the author to convince the reader to take their side by using emotions, logic, and evidence. However, argument writing is much more balanced. Argument writing is about analyzing and debating a topic with several claims for one side while recognizing that there are reasonable counterclaims for the opposing side.

In today's classrooms, there is particular emphasis on students' ability to write sound arguments. In fact, this is a key shift found in the work of the Common Core State Standards (CCSS). In the CCSS, developing argument writing starts in kindergarten through fifth grade, where the term "opinion writing" is used for students to begin supporting a point of view with facts and details.

This picture book is designed to give educators a tool to share with children that will help identify the differences between persuasive and argument writing, as each is often mistaken for the other. With rubrics, high-quality student samples, and guidance, children like Melvin Fargo will confidently develop their writing craft and find much success with their newly defined writing endeavors.

References include:

National Governors Association Center for Best Practices & Council of Chief State School Officers. (2010). Common Core State Standards for English language arts and literacy in history/social studies, science, and technical subjects: Appendix A. Washington, DC: Authors.

It was the second day of school
and the teacher said real stern,
"The honeymoon is over.
It's time for you to learn!"

Melvin Fargo

Writes to Argue and Persuade

TOOLS FOR TEACHERS

Written by Lisa Rivard, PhD and Illustrated by Jeff Covieo

FERNE PRESS

Melvin Fargo Writes to Argue and Persuade
Copyright © 2014 by Lisa Rivard

Layout and cover design by Jacqueline L. Challiss Hill
Illustrations by Jeff Covieo
Illustrations created with graphic and digital art

Printed in Canada

Summary: Fifth grader Melvin Fargo is tasked to write an argument essay and a persuasive essay.

Library of Congress Cataloging-in-Publication Data
    Rivard, Lisa
    Melvin Fargo Writes to Argue and Persuade/Lisa Rivard–First Edition
    ISBN-13: 978-1-938326-23-3
    1. Essay writing. 2. Elementary school. 3. Teacher tool. 4. Common Core State Standards.
    I. Rivard, Lisa II. Title
    Library of Congress Control Number: 2013956667

FERNE PRESS

Ferne Press is an imprint of Nelson Publishing & Marketing
366 Welch Road, Northville, MI 48167
www.nelsonpublishingandmarketing.com
(248) 735-0418

To those who inspire creativity in our classrooms. Thank you for all you do!

"Your college days are near!
Only eight more years to go.
Let's get down to business.
Let me teach you what I know."

Oh no! Writing homework!
A very lengthy task
that requires a bit of thought
and for me to take a stance.

My job is to ponder
the question on the chart.
Take a firm position
and write it from the heart.

Should kids choose
their own bedtime?

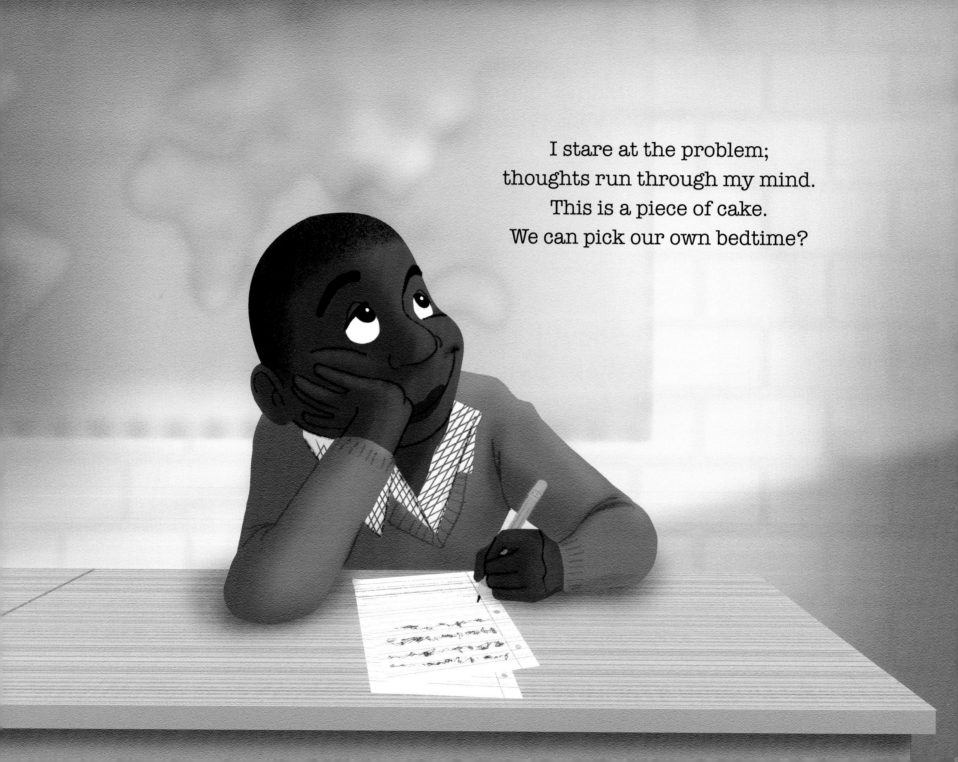

I stare at the problem;
thoughts run through my mind.
This is a piece of cake.
We can pick our own bedtime?

Yes! Yes indeed,
kids should stay up late.
As long as we get up for school,
there's nothing to debate.

I form my point of view
and include my opinion.
I follow with my reasons
why I take this position.

I stay up very late
and write a whole page.

I address it to my parents,
the audience to engage.

I turn in my paper
and think I'm good to go.
But near the end of the day,
I hear, "Melvin Fargo."

My first task is done;
I persuaded the reader's mind.
She says, "Please write to argue
and include some logical finds."

PERSUADE?

ARGUE?

I didn't know the difference,
a variation of the two.
I had written to persuade
and now I must argue?

To argue is a bit different:
I still state my point of view
and address the same audience
with real facts I include.

I study many texts
and begin to compare.

I group like ideas.
A new opinion is clear.

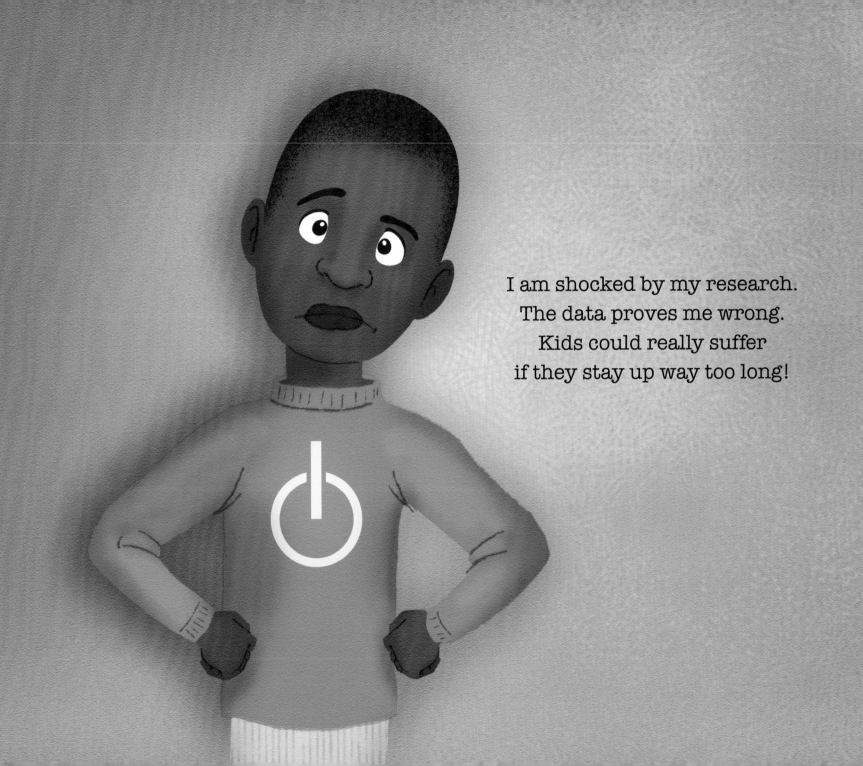

I am shocked by my research.
The data proves me wrong.
Kids could really suffer
if they stay up way too long!

My fingers are quite busy;
there's so much to include.

Data, charts, graphs, and tables,
things that I can prove!

I reach a logical conclusion
and organize the mound.
I need to cite my work,
give credit to details found.

Before I finish my paper,
I use the rubric tool.

I check off all I need,
then I'm ready for school.

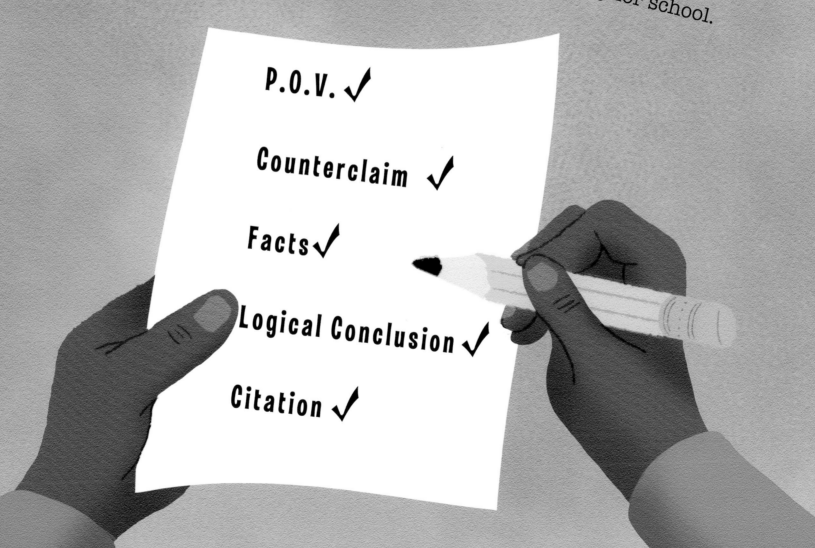

An entire day goes by
before I learn my fate.

"Come here, Melvin Fargo."
Would I be proud or just deflate?

"Congrats, Mr. Fargo!
I'm extremely impressed.
You persuaded me at first,
then passed the argument test."

I can't believe my ears!
I did something right!
Before I celebrate,
"Here's your homework for tonight!"

No, no, not more!
I'm exhausted to the max.
I stayed up all night long
for a grade that would pass.

I look at the note
and it says in bold ink,
Your homework tonight
is to practice what you think!

Turn the TV off at eight.

Shut your book at nine.

Get eight hours of sleep

and get to school on time!

~ Melvin's Persuasive Letter ~

Dear Parents,

As long as kids get up on time for school it doesn't matter if they stay up late. Kids need more time to do things they want to do. They already have to do homework, sports, and take care of pets or little brothers and sisters.

For one thing, kids need more time after dinner to relax and watch television and play games. If parents tell kids when to go to bed, they may make it too early to be able to do fun things.

Additionally, if kids go to bed when they want, they would have more time to study or read a book. Maybe if kids could go to bed when they want, they will be more responsible and go right to sleep.

Considering all of this, I think kids should choose their own bedtime.

Melvin Fargo

~ Melvin's Argument Letter ~

Dear Parents,

As night falls, kids of the world often whine and cry about going to bed on time. Kids just do not have enough time between school and bedtime to get all their activities finished. There is just not enough time for video games, chatting with friends, eating dinner, watching TV, and homework, too.

But although it sounds like a great idea to stay up late to have some free time, new research says it may not be very healthy for kids to choose their own bedtime. Kids in school need between eight and twelve hours of sleep each night.

Recently, a survey by Dr. Elise Thomas about sleeping was given to 1,000 girls and boys. And though kids are famous for not wanting to go to sleep, 70% said they wished they could get more of it. 71% of kids said they felt sort of sleepy or very sleepy when it's time to wake up for school. Research also shows that getting a good night's sleep may be the very best thing to improve a student's academic performance in school.

So even though staying up late sounds really fun and exciting, kids may just want to reconsider this bright idea! Kids that want to be the best they can be really should shut off the lights and go to bed!

Melvin Fargo

Lisa Rivard was raised in New Baltimore, Michigan. Throughout her life, she has enjoyed working with children in many different capacities, including as a teacher, coach, and principal. She earned her teaching degree from Michigan State University and her administration degree from Oakland University. Most recently, Lisa completed a PhD in Instructional Technology from Wayne State University. Currently, Lisa is employed as a Language Arts Consultant and assists regional schools in developing effective literacy plans. For more information about Lisa, please visit her website www.lisarivardbooks.com.

Jeff Covieo has been drawing since he could hold a pencil and hasn't stopped since. He has a BFA in photography from College for Creative Studies in Michigan and works in the commercial photography field, though drawing and illustration have been his avocation for years. *Melvin Fargo Writes to Argue and Persuade* is the eighth book he has illustrated.